Alaska Animal Antics

Animals, wild and tame,
from moose to mosquitoes
and their involvement with Alaskans.

Elverda Lincoln

PO Box 221974 Anchorage, Alaska 99522-1974

ISBN 1-888125-90-X

Library of Congress Catalog Card Number: 2001098237

Manufactured in the United States of America.

Dedication

Enjoy!!!

The frontier may have been conquered by strong men but it was the women who held the family together. They endured struggles, happiness, hardships, and disappointments in order to make a life for all.

This book is dedicated to all Alaskan women and to all my fellow writers of the TaleSpinners and the Mat-Su Adult Writer's Group. I thank them for encouraging me to keep writing, and offering valuable advice and critique.

I would like to give special thanks to eleven-year-old Sam Ryden of Wasilla for his expertise in drawing the cartoons.

A special thank you to Marthy Johnson for her expertise in bringing the words of this book to their final form.

Elwerda Lincoln

TABLE OF CONTENTS

Dedication 3

THE BON MARCHE BAG .... Margaret Swensen 7

THE BEAR .... Margaret Heaven 9

TEETH MARKS IN THE BUTTER .... Elizabeth White 12

SURVIVOR .... Cara Lou Lilly 14

STAR .... Carol Stewart 18

SQUIRRELS IN THE CABIN .... Maureen Kelly 21

SHREWS .... Elverda Lincoln 24

SHE TRIED .... Elvera Corkery 26

SCARED .... Marilyn Cook 27

ROUND AND ROUND .... Marilyn Cook 28

RETIREMENT PROJECT .... Elverda Lincoln 29

PORCUPINES .... Elverda Lincoln 31

PIGS ON THE LOOSE .... Mary Knutson 33

OUR ALASKA OUTHOUSE .... Darlene Robinson 35

OINKER .... Elverda Lincoln 37

NOT YET .... Myrtle Gislason 40

NORTHERN CHICKENS .... Elverda Lincoln 41

NEVER AGAIN .... Margaret Heaven 45

MOVING BRANCH .... Carol Stewart 48

THE MIGHTY HUNTERS .... Elverda Lincoln 49

MEMORIES OF A SHOPPER .... Elverda Lincoln 50

THE MAGGOT SANDWICH .... Elverda Lincoln 53

LIFE ON THE FARM .... Elverda Lincoln 55

JUDY'S STORIES .... Judy Fielding 57

I WANTED A SALMON .... Mary Harvey 59

HOOKS AND LURES .... Joyce Cook 60

FRIGHTENED MOOSE .... Jeanene Buccaria 62

FRIENDLY PEOPLE AND MOSQUITOES .. Mary Harvey 64

FRIEDA AND THE GOOSE .... Carol Stewart 65

DOMINIC .... Carol Stewart 67

CYRUS AND BLESSED .... Carol Stewart 68

CAMPGROUND PORCUPINE .... Phyllis Hassinger 70

BUGS, SNAILS, AND PUPPY DOG TAILS . Maureen Kelly 72

BEAR WATCH .... Joyce Cook 77

BARN SHOWER .... Mildred Ulrich 79

BACKYARD BEAR .... Mary Harvey 81

BABY .... Evelyn McNair 82

ARNOLD .... Darlene Robinson 84

ALASKA BEGINNINGS .... Koreen Robinson 87

A FOWL ROMANCE .... June Robinette 89

ALASKA BEAR ENCOUNTERS .... Judy Shelton 91

FROZEN .... Mary Knutson 96

THE BON MARCHE BAG
Margaret Swensen

Rose and her husband were married for more than forty years; consequently she knew how Tony hated to shop. Since it was near the Christmas season and the weather was bad she coaxed and pleaded with him to go shopping with her. He finally consented, but complained all the way to the Dimond Mall. She told him it would be fine if he wanted to wait in the car.

"I won't be long, dear," she said. It had started to snow hard by the time she scurried from the car into the mall. He settled back with a book.

A dilapidated Volkswagen bus caught his eye as it pulled into a nearby parking space. He paused a moment from his reading to watch a woman get out of the van, give six children firm orders about staying in the car, and hurry into the mall. As he watched, the van jostled back and forth. He could imagine the kids scuffling and jumping inside. One of the children rolled down the steamy window and a big, screeching tabby cat jumped out into the wet snow. Just as he hit the ground, another car pulled into the lot. The snow-blinded driver unknowingly ran over the cat, killing it instantly.

As Tony watched, the harried mother returned to the van, her arms full of packages. Screams and frantic crying assailed her as she opened the door. She got into the van and instantly got out again with an empty Bon Marche bag, from the sophisticated ladies department store in Seattle. She placed the dead cat in the bag, deposited it carefully next to a nearby garbage dumpster, returned to the van full of crying children and drove away.

Tony was completely fascinated as a very rich looking Lincoln car pulled up and a tiny frail woman dressed in furs got out and approached the Bon Marche bag. She looked stealthily around, then snatched up the bag. Assuming she had found a treasure she stole a look into the bag, saw the contents, and fainted dead away in the snow. Her husband raced around the car to give her aid. Seeing she was still alive he dashed into the mall to call 911. Moments later, a shrieking ambulance, lights flashing, pulled into the parking lot. Attendants loaded the unconscious woman onto a stretcher and into the ambulance. Just as they closed the doors, one of the attendants scooped the bag into the cab with him.

By this time Tony, waiting for his wife, was starting to chuckle. As the ambulance slowly pulled onto the street, it suddenly weaved recklessly in the traffic, managed to pull over to the curb. The Bon Marche bag was hurled into the snow.

The wife returned to hear her husband chuckling to himself.

"What's so funny, dear?" she asked.

"Oh nothing. I was just thinking how much fun it was waiting for you while you shopped. Did you get everything you needed?"

"Yes, dear. We can go home now."

THE BEAR
Margaret Heaven

My family left Alaska in 1954 when I was twelve
years old. Looking out of the back window of our
car as we drove toward the Matanuska River
Bridge on what is now the Old Glenn Highway I promised
Palmer I would return. We were driving to Anchorage to
catch a plane to the States, en route to Massachusetts for a
year, and then on to somewhere else.

In 1966 I returned to Alaska, home to my beautiful Matanuska
Valley. Though I had lived in Palmer as a child, it was to
Wasilla that I returned to live as an adult. Even the Palmer-
Wasilla school rivalry could not keep me from accepting a
teaching job there, our basketball team's archenemy.

That first year in Wasilla, I rented a downstairs apartment in town. Another teacher, Lila Cooper, who was from Anchorage, was my roommate. When spring came, the desire to live with space between me and my neighbors became an obsession.

Four miles south of Wasilla, just off the newly rebuilt Knik Road, I bought a five-acre parcel of land complete with a small cabin. In the spring of 1967, as the school year ended, Lila and I moved our meager belongings, my cat, dog and parakeet out of our apartment and into my cabin.

That summer Lila went to visit her sister. I enjoyed time alone in my little home in the woods. The dog and I took walks for miles along old trails. An opening in the lower part of the kitchen door permitted the dog to come and go at will. Tending the garden, picking raspberries, strawberries, and currants, sometimes by myself and sometimes with a friend, kept me busy.

In the summer of 1968, Lila and another friend both left the state to visit relatives Outside. I again enjoyed the summer by myself. Many bears lived around the Wasilla area that summer. As I shopped for groceries in Teeland's Store or when we met at the post office, people talked of seeing them in various areas. Normally, I love to see wildlife as close to where I live as possible, even bears. Being by myself, I began to think I should be prepared to defend myself if necessary.

My brother had let me bring his 30.06 rifle to Alaska and I decided I should do some target shooting, just to be safe. I purchased extra bullets and started practicing. A target was set up east of the cabin, and from there I practiced shooting, from the front porch, from the back porch, from the jeep, and from the roof. I was ready! Any bear that came around the cabin was doomed.

My unloaded rifle hung above the fireplace, but now I decided to keep it in a corner near the door, loaded, in case a bear came close.

One night in August, my dog started growling and looking down our driveway. She growled low in her throat and I knew it was not some animal that might normally be there, like a moose, rabbit or a squirrel. Peering into the darkness I couldn't see a thing. The dog kept growling. Quickly grabbing my loaded rifle I went out on the porch.

In the tall grass, near a clump of trees in my circular driveway I heard a rustling. I hollered, "If you are a bear, you better leave! I don't want to shoot you, but I will." I didn't want to kill anything. I just didn't want to be eaten.

There was no answer from a bear or anything else and nothing moved. The dog kept growling and her hair stood up even straighter. I yelled, "Get out of here!" and aimed the rifle above where I thought the animal must be. I fired, listened to the silence and kept my rifle ready. Then I raised it, ready to shoot again.

Suddenly I heard, "Don't shoot!"

A man stood up. It was LeRoi Heaven, a man whom I was dating and later married. He had parked at the end of the driveway and was planning to scare me. Well, he did. But not as much as I scared him. He has never tried to scare me again when he thought I might have a gun handy.

TEETH MARKS IN THE BUTTER
Elizabeth White

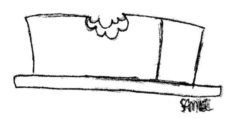

Years ago, when our kids were still at home, we lived in Anchorage, in an A-frame house. The back part had an addition with a flat roof. A triangular window in the end of the original section was a few inches above the addition.

Our children had a small white terrier named Sandy, who slept and played with them. Many squirrels lived around our wooded area and they ran up and down the roof teasing the dog. Of course, she barked.

On bread-baking day the squirrels would sit on the ledge of the odd-shaped window and chatter. The odor of the fresh-smelling bread seemed to attract them, and at the same time they were enjoying themselves by scolding the dog.

One day, Connie, our family baker, set some fresh bread on the table to cool, then opened the back door to let some heat escape from the kitchen. When the family was sitting in the living room, they heard a noise. Through the doorway to the kitchen they saw a squirrel eating the cooling bread. Later, they even found teeth marks in the butter.

The squirrels pestered and upset the dog until they had her

so nervous and excitable, no one could control her. This seemed to be great sport for these bushy-tailed rodents.

One day I was on the porch watching Sandy chase a squirrel which she had caught by the tail. The dog ran across the yard like this until the tail slipped out of her mouth. The squirrel climbed the nearest tree and chattered at the dog what sounded like a laugh.

Many trees grew along a steep bank behind our house. One tree growing out from the bank was leaning at a 45 degree angle. Sandy chased a squirrel up that tree. The dog followed the squirrel to the end of the tree and then couldn't get down. I helped her but this experience didn't discourage her from ignoring the antics of the squirrels.

We have fond memories of that house.

SURVIVOR
Cara Lou Lilly

In early 1980, I cooked at Gabert's Fish Camp on beautiful Alexander Creek, located thirty miles northwest of Anchorage, Alaska. People came from far and near to hunt and fish in this pristine area. The lodge stayed open from May through September. You could make reservations for a day, overnight, by the week or month. That was the summer my husband and I helped save an injured eagle.

My job was to feed twenty to thirty guests daily, consisting of a hearty breakfast, lunch, and dinner. They needed plenty of energy for the long fishing day as well as to fight mosquitoes who were out in full force.

Bob, my husband, worked a week on and a week off for Alyeska Pipeline at Prudhoe Bay. An avid pilot, he enjoyed flying his PA12 Super Cub to Gabert's Lodge when he was home. He also had his own boat at the lodge. When there were few tourists at the lodge, we made many trips on the water.

September rolled around and this was a fabulous time for us. Fall colors were out. Hunting season was open. Ducks were flying, and hungry rainbow trout and even late-returning silver salmon choked the rivers.

We loaded the airboat with fishing gear and a rifle in high hopes of obtaining a record moose trophy. As we rounded a bend some distance downstream, we noticed a bald eagle hopping around, having trouble trying to fly. We proceeded to our favorite fishing spot and decided to check the condition of the eagle on our way back to the lodge.

By the time fishing was over it was late and we had more than an hour's ride back to the lodge. We knew it was colder on the water when the sun went down.

As we passed the clearing, the eagle was in the same place, hopping and trying to become airborne. As we continued downstream my thoughts were of the bird. I commented to my husband that the eagle wouldn't survive the winter. He agreed.

The next morning I suggested we return to the area to see how the eagle was faring. The bird seemed more agitated than the day before. Bob and I discussed what we could or should do for this beautiful creature. From our observation he appeared to be fully grown, four to five years old, with a white head and tail, and a yellow beak and eyes. My husband informed me that the law said a person couldn't even have in their possession a bald eagle feather, much less the whole bird.

We returned to the lodge and made phone calls to the Department of Fish and Game in Anchorage. They gave us permission to retrieve the eagle and transport it back to Anchorage for medical treatment.

We again loaded the air boat for our last trip downstream. Sure enough, as we rounded the bend near the clearing, the eagle was in the same condition as we had previously noted. From a distance, he looked like a child fishing from shore. Throwing anchor, Bob, with his king salmon net in hand, jumped out of the boat. The chase was on. The frightened eagle tried flying across the stream. Since he wasn't able to get airborne, he crashed in the middle and drifted downstream. We returned to the boat and drifted also. By the time we caught up to him, the eagle was trying to climb up the riverbank. As Bob got closer, the eagle was searching for an escape. There was none. The eagle stared at us with cold, penetrating eyes, sending shivers up and down my spine. I yelled at Bob to hurry and put the net over the eagle's head. The bird was in such a state of fright he didn't notice what was happening to him.

Soon he was rolled up into the net, and hissing. If he escaped we would have been in bad trouble. We wasted no time getting the eagle and net rolled into a tarp, wrapping it with duct tape, and lifting him into the boat.

Before heading back to the lodge, we returned to the clearing where the chase had begun. We found a moose spine picked clean and a trail which led to an area with tall grass tramped down. Feathers and black bear fur were everywhere —evidence the two had fought over moose remains.

Safely back at the lodge, we put the ten-pound eagle into a warm sauna room until we were ready for the thirty-mile trip to Anchorage. We took scores of pictures.

The airplane was loaded with our gear. The only place for the huge bird was on my lap, in the cramped back seat. He was so restricted in his blanket of net, tarp, and duct tape, he didn't move. Pilot Bob was up front, winging our way to Lake Hood near Anchorage. Every now and then he shouted, asking if all was fine. Both the bird and I were speechless with fright. As we landed I could see our old pickup waiting to take our load home.

At the animal hospital, Dr. Scott took over. As he pulled off the tape and unrolled the tarp, he let us know what a fine job we had done. He also confirmed our theory as to what had taken place. The flight feathers had been lost in the fight over the moose spine. They don't grow back unless molted naturally. He implanted feathers from an available dried wing the following day. The repaired bird was then put into a flight cage for rehabilitation until the following spring. Bob and I visited the eagle periodically during the winter. When we did, he hissed at us. I am sure he remembered we were responsible for his confinement.

We gained much information from Dr. Scott as he worked with the injured eagle. Treatment for the battered wing included "imping," the practice of repairing and replacing broken flight feathers. This process was done by trimming off the damaged portion of the old feather and attaching a new feather that had been cut to the proper length. With the hollow shaft of each feather exposed, bamboo pins and glue were used to join the two feathers together. They were then wrapped with thread and extra glue for reinforcement.

In the spring the eagle molted naturally before it was released into the wild. Molting was a gradual process. Flight feathers aren't lost all at once, consequently the eagle was never flightless during this time. Dr. Scott wrote an article for veterinary publications of this rare occurrence, which had never been documented before.

The eagle soared.

STAR
Carol Stewart

Star, the horse, was about ten years old when we acquired her from a friend who had rescued her from a field of foxtail. The horse was trying to nurse a foal, although she was quite sick. We soon found out she was a very difficult animal. The vet did surgery on her mouth, which had been injured by sharp foxtail weeds.

Our fourteen-year-old daughter, Susan, wanted to ride the horse in the worst way. She went to the library and checked out a book on equestrian riding and found out one could train a horse with leg movements. A bit was not needed. It took most of the summer to work with the animal. Eventually, Star learned her mouth didn't hurt anymore, and accepted the bit.

It was two miles from our place to the main highway, where Susan rode the bus to school. Every morning she took care of the animals, including milking the cow and saddling the horse. I suggested she give the horse a small amount of her breakfast grain, then tie up her reins when she got to the bus stop, and the horse would come home. Sure enough, the horse came home on a dead run and into the barn to get her remaining grain. I tried to train her to meet Susan at the bus stop in the afternoon, but she wasn't about to leave the warm barn and food.

Star soon learned she didn't have to be tied up while grazing in the immediate area. It didn't matter since we were the only family living in that neck of the woods. Occasionally, I lost sight of her, and hollered, "Star, where are you?" The horse then lifted her head and looked up like a five-year-old saying, "Here I am, Mom." At dinnertime we called her and she trotted home to get her food.

A bunch of ladies who were at my house for a meeting noticed the horse and remarked she was such a nice horse and never ran away.

I said to them, "Do you want to see something funny? Star, dinner."

The horse perked up her head and trotted to the house. The next thing I knew, she pushed her way into the open garage door. I heard thumping and clumping. The horse was trying to climb up the stairs to the kitchen to get her dinner. Since I had called her from the kitchen she thought that was where her dinner was. The women were impressed as I led her back down the stairs.

One of these women had five kids. Since Susan was soon going off to college, she sold Star to the family, but the horse never made up to those kids. They couldn't ride her or get near enough to feed her. The only thing they could do was put food in the middle of the pasture and when everyone went to bed Star ate. Susan bought her back when she returned home.

Susan taught Star to give rides to small children. The horse was originally a fierce, bucking mare because she was afraid of everybody, but she became as tame as a big pussycat

She liked kids, in fact, she walked along with her swayback, and if the riders slid around or were close to slipping off, she gave a push in the right direction to keep them on. When the riders were on her back, she walked in one direction, sometimes trotting, then turned around and went back. She always stopped in front of Susan and the other children because she knew the other kids wanted to ride too.

Late one fall, in hunting season, my husband decided to take Star moose hunting. He comes from a line of horse trainers and breakers in the Lower 48. He whopped the horse on her ear and the top of her head to get her attention, threw the saddle on her back, got on, and started kicking her in the ribs to make her go. Where he was kicking, the horse was trained to back up. Susan and I watched from the porch of the house as rider and horse backed down the driveway. They were going and going, and my husband was getting madder and madder because the horse wouldn't do what he wanted. Susan and I laughed and laughed at the show. I finally gave in and hollered at him, "If you would quit kicking her and use the reins you will get much further. Let your legs hang loose. You are telling her to go backwards." My husband didn't like to do this too well, but decided this might work better than going backwards through the woods to see the moose that got away.

Originally, Susan had got the horse because she wanted to take horse showmanship as a 4-H project. Star was getting old, kind of swaybacked, big hooves, one ear hanging down, clunky-looking with kind of a pretty face for a horse. Susan had trained her well, to walk, stop, and trot. At the showmanship trials, the judge walked by to see how the horse was behaving. Star went to sleep standing on her feet which caused her stomach to sag more and more. Then Susan reached over and poked the horse in the stomach. Star pulled her tummy up and was pretty again for the judge. She got all the purple and blue ribbons because she behaved so well. No one knew she really went to sleep.

Star lived to be twenty-five years old. She was put out to pasture at Susan's farm, where she kept old pet horses to live out their lives.

SQUIRRELS IN THE CABIN
Maureen Kelly

My husband, daughter and I were delighted with our new abode, located out in the wilds of the Tanana River, twenty miles south of North Pole near Fairbanks. Our move from Juneau was a massive undertaking. All of our possessions had to be packed into our station wagon, precious items we thought we had to have to set up housekeeping.

The cabin was made of rough-hewn logs from the property. The building was constructed when the logs were green. When they dried out and shrank, there were great open spaces between the logs. These spaces were chinked with fiberglass insulation. Frost heaves caused the cabin to lean, a common condition in the north.

Upon entering the front and only door, to our immediate left was a large picture window. A gas stove which rarely worked was on the left wall and a coat and boot area was just behind the door. The kitchen and dining area took up the rest of the floor space. A stairway was stuck to the far corner wall behind the gluttonous wood stove. I say gluttonous because someone had previously burned coal and left its poor little black belly with great cracks in it. Uncontrolled heat escaped from these cracks.

Upstairs were two small loft bedrooms and a bathroom tucked under an A-frame roof. The bathroom had plumbing, which we were thankful for, especially during the cold winter months. An automatic washing machine was also situated in this crowded bathroom.

The cookstove was fueled with propane and worked great until the temperature dropped to minus forty degrees. That was just too cold for the outside fuel tank. Severe cold caused the gas to freeze in the regulator; consequently, it wouldn't flow through the fuel line. Then I learned to cook roasts and breads in the wood-burning stove.

One morning I happened to glance toward the window and saw insulation flying away from the cabin, and the wind wasn't even blowing. I found that a woodpecker was pulling and tossing it out while snooping for bugs.

One day, I was tending the neighbor's little children and caught them pulling out insulation, too. Of course they got a lecture from me not to do this. It was odd to see outdoors through the walls. I could imagine hunting moose from inside the cabin. Then a pair of squirrels burrowed in between the plastic sheeting and insulation under the eaves, just above my kitchen cupboards. I heard the rustlings up there and upon investigating, had a front row view of mama, papa, and large family of baby squirrels. I watched the antics and rapid growth of the babies for that whole season. This was entertainment for our family. We didn't disturb them, but always felt a bit squeamish while they were there with just a sheet of plastic separating our two families.

We didn't have off-the-floor beds for quite some time at this cabin; we slept on firm slabs of thick foam. On several mornings, I awoke to find my blankets frozen to the wall and floor. Condensation caused by cooking, heating water, and drying clothes rose from the first floor to the upper area. That made it difficult to smooth out the blankets. I kept my feet close to my body at night.

I built a bird feeder on the kitchen windowsill which attracted many kinds of birds. Chickadees and woodpeckers loved the suet, bread crumbs and birdseed that I provided daily.

The floor of the porch is where I built a tiered box garden out of old railroad ties. I worked hard for days, gleaning soil from the forest floor and from overturned tree roots to fill the boxes. My garden of vegetables, flowers, and tomatoes under plastic, yielded enough for a summer of fresh fare. The satisfaction that I could garden so far north was important also.

In spite of modern conveniences, there were still enough rough and raw conditions that made my living in this little log cabin a childhood dream come true.

The dream continues in this great land in the North.

SHREWS
Elverda Lincoln

When we arrived in Alaska in the spring of 1950, a small-two room log cabin was our first home. It hadn't been lived in for quite some time, and as a result, nature was returning it to its original state. Brush and wild grasses had reclaimed the yard, and mice had taken over the dirty cabin.

Our landlady, a pleasant kind woman, who lived half a mile from us, visited us often to see how we cheechakos were adjusting to life in the country. The first time she made her appearance she said to me, "Have you noticed any shrews around yet?"

"Shrews," I exclaimed, "What are those?"

"They look like mice," she replied, "They have long tails and have more pointed noses than mice. They measure from three to six inches long, from nose to tail. You will notice they are nervous, panicky animals, with a ferocious appetite. If they don't eat their own weight every three hours they will starve to death."

I listened intently to every word.

She continued, "That is why I came over to see you, to

warn you of the five-gallon bucket buried near the well. The top of the bucket is level with the top of the ground. A shrew will fall into the bucket and can't get out, soon another one will fall in, one will eat the other. This process can go on forever. By the way, count the tails, and you will know how many fell in."

She then was on her way, after observing and commenting on some of the improvements made to make the cabin more livable.

Every day for a week I peered into the bucket and observed three tails. The more I thought of this method the more I was not impressed. I feared my two-year-old-son might fall into the bucket. For safety, I filled it with dirt and left no evidence it was ever there.

Common mouse traps did the job from then on, and I assure you, the shrews thought they owned the cabin. During the night I could hear the traps snap. Throughout the summer I eliminated many of them, but when winter came, new families moved in, and the process started all over again. I never found all the holes they used to enter the cabin. The building, made of logs, provided gaps small enough for a shrew to seek food and warm shelter. With constant chinking I must have missed the tiniest of openings.

I was determined to win this battle. The next possible solution was to acquire a cat. The neighbors across the road blessed us with a kitten, which was named Bobo. For some months the cute little feline thought shrews were toys, but as it grew, instinct took over, and the cat soon learned to work for his keep. Then the shrew killer left the dead little beasts on the outside doorstep, for all to admire. That was fine with me. Dead shrews were better than live ones.

SHE TRIED
Elvera Corkery

Summer in Alaska is the time for relatives and friends to visit relatives and friends here in Alaska. So it was with a friend of mine, who took many scenic trips with an acquaintance, who made her first visit to this great state.

On one of their trips along the coast they noticed groups of people with long-handled nets scooping something out of the water. Some were standing waist-deep in the water. The guest wanted to know what they were doing. Her friend explained they were hooligan fishing, and then educated her on how, where, and when this is done. She also explained that in other parts of the country hooligan are known as grunion or smelt.

Of course, the guest was excited about this challenge and wanted to try it herself. They had no nets or hip boots with them, so it seemed impossible for them to join in the fun. Then the grossly overweight guest had a bright idea. She hid out of sight in the bushes, took off her bloomers, tied a knot in the end of each leg, waded into the water, and scooped like all the other fishermen. She caught more hooligan that way than anyone else. She was elated. As they drove off with their loot, they wondered what the other fishermen told their friends and family about the newest styles in dipnets.

SCARED
Marilyn Cook

In the early 1990s, I went with my husband, Dennis, and another couple on a long-awaited fishing trip to Trapper Creek, about a hundred miles north of Anchorage, Alaska. Each couple had their own airboat. Upon arrival at our favorite spot on the bank of a creek, we enjoyed a picnic lunch. It was a beautiful, sunny day, with just enough of a breeze to keep the voracious mosquitoes at bay. Before we proceeded back on the water, we two women made a nature call. We hiked toward some bushes on the crest of a small hill and assumed a position.

As luck would have it, a bear came strolling over the top of the hill. Squatting there, we were now face to face with this wild woodland bruin. What a surprise! The bear made an abrupt turnaround and ran upriver from whence he'd come. I outran my companion back to our airboat, yelling about bears. Speedily, I yanked up the anchor, threw it into the boat, barely missing Dennis. My husband stopped me from taking the boat. True to the nature of men, he demanded directions so he and his buddy could go see the bear with their own eyes.

I told him where to go.

ROUND AND ROUND
Marilyn Cook

A few years ago I was employed as an Alaska State Trooper in the judicial system. We picked up prisoners and delivered them to the doctor, to various prisons, and other duties as they were assigned.

One day we received a call to arrest a man and a woman at their home. They had locked themselves inside the house with their three children. Two large black vicious-looking guard dogs were tied up, near the doors in the front and backyards. How does an officer respond to this? Creativity was called for.

I noticed a heavy metal truck wheel in the front yard, so I teased one of the dogs to get him to follow me as I ran round and round the wheel.

This caused the chain to get shorter and shorter, until the dog's head was snubbed up tight to the ground. Then officers were able to complete the arrest.

RETIREMENT PROJECT
Elverda Lincoln

My daughter and son-in-law were snowmobiling in a remote area north of Talkeetna, Alaska. After an exhausting day on the trail, they ended up at a restaurant for a hot meal and to warm up their tired bones. While waiting for their hamburgers to arrive, they became engaged in a conversation with a local old-timer.

One of the stories they enjoyed the most was about two women, recently retired from secretarial jobs in Anchorage, who decided to live in a cabin in the woods. The ladies were tired of the rat race of Anchorage, the noise, traffic, and hassle of city living. Concerned with what they were going to do with their time while living in a cabin, they discussed raising twenty-five chickens. They would have fresh fryers to eat, eggs to trade and sell, and to use for their own needs, like omelets, deviled eggs and angel food cakes. Their plan was carried out.

In time, the chicks grew to fryer size. The ladies knew they had to butcher some of the birds, but neither woman knew much about this gruesome task. One of them had grown up on a farm in the Midwest. She at least remembered how her parents performed this ritual. They held the chicken by its legs, laid the neck on a stump and chopped off its head, then dropped the chicken on the ground. It flopped around until it was dead. The other lady had no idea how to kill a chicken and dreaded the day she would have to learn.

One sunny day in late summer they decided the time had come for this event to take place. The inexperienced butchers made preparations to keep the bloody mess out of their clearing. The nearby woods was the scene of this carnage.

The cabin, wired for electricity, had no water available except what they hauled from a nearby spring. They knew that when the chickens were flopping around on the ground blood would be splattered here and there and maybe some would end up on their clothes. It was a chore washing bloody jeans and shirts by hand so they decided to wear only their underwear while killing the chickens. Washing blood off themselves was easier than washing clothes.

When the job was finished, they put the chicken's bodies in a wheelbarrow and rolled them back to their cabin. They were just coming into their clearing when the meter reader drove into their yard. He saw two women wearing bloody underwear coming out of the woods with a wheelbarrow full of dead something or other.

The frightened man made a quick U-turn and left the yard, not bothering to read the meter!

PORCUPINES
Elverda Lincoln

Soon after arriving in the Matanuska Valley in 1950 we settled down in a small cabin. A friendly neighbor family invited us to dinner one evening. The main course was porcupine. I'm the type of person who is willing to sample any unfamiliar food. The meat was delicious. It tasted like chicken. In fact, my husband was so impressed with the delicate taste he vowed he would kill one for dinner. A few weeks later a porcupine ventured into our yard and he proceeded to do the deed.

How do you skin a porcupine? Very carefully. He nailed the upside down porky to a tree and when he was finished he came into the cabin. "Come out here and tell me what you think?" The porky looked like a baby there on the tree.

"I'm not eating that," I stammered. He felt the same way I did. He never killed a porcupine again, nor did we ever eat another.

When we moved into the cabin, our three-year-old, Roger, went to the outside biffy one morning. He came running to the cabin hollering, "Mommy, there's a big animal out there. He's going to get me."

'Well, come on, show me." I took his tiny hand and there in the path was a porcupine, waddling along in his unique way.

Roger wanted to keep it to show Daddy. We took a wash tub, turned it over the animal, and shared the experience with Daddy that evening before releasing the spiny critter back into the woods.

A year later we moved to a larger cabin closer to Wasilla. Our landlady told us there were strange animals living under the cabin. We heard loud, grunting noises, but never knew what caused them until one day we saw two porcupines come out from under the cabin.

By observing these creatures we learned their quills point to the rear, while the nose and face are covered with short hair and whiskers. An adult porky stands about eighteen inches high and has a six to ten inch tail. They are vegetarian, and will eat most anything, including garden vegetables, tree bark, boards, and handles of axes (they contain salt left by human hands), berries and mushrooms. It's the only animal in the woods that can be killed with a stick or rifle butt, so if a person is lost he can survive by eating porcupine.

Three years later we moved to our homestead, and by that time had acquired two large collie dogs, Lassie and Ranger. They both were inquisitive and managed to bark and nip at a porcupine. Consequently, both ended up with quills in their noses. Lassie learned her lesson from this experience, but Ranger never did. Many times we could hear Ranger near the barn whining and moaning. We knew he'd had another bout with a porcupine and was in great pain. I sat on the dog to hold it still while my husband pulled out the quills one by one. If every quill is not removed it can work itself into the innards of the dog and eventually cause its death.

In frontier days trappers, miners, and homesteaders experienced lean times living in the wilds. A tasty meal of fried porcupine helped them survive. Today it is against the law to kill a porcupine.

PIGS ON THE LOOSE
Mary Knutson

t was one of those especially nice hot days in the summer of 1992. This particular day, I was staying home with my oldest son and his family, who lived in our basement apartment.

I spent the morning planting raspberry starts received from a friend, then cleaned up and left for a few hours. I came home to a real three-ring circus. Here was my big-as-a-barn seven-months-pregnant daughter-in-law Kim, running around the yard with a rake in her hands chasing two huge full-grown pigs. At the same time, she was trying to get a four-year-old boy and a three-year-old girl to go back in the house. The children wanted to enjoy the fun also.

Grabbing a hoe and joining the ruckus I helped her chase those pigs all over our little corner of the world and back again. The more we tried to get them out of the yard, the more determined they were to stay. They made several trips through the garden, which made Kim furious.

My particular frustration came when she chased the pigs out of the garden, because they headed straight to my newly planted raspberries and lay down. I wanted to kill both pigs. When I finally got them out of the raspberries, they ran in the front yard and lay down in the kids' little swimming pool, poking holes in it with their sharp hooves.

Kim and I phoned everyone we could to find out who the runaways belonged to. I contacted my closest neighbor, Elverda Lincoln, who helped make calls. We called the State

Troopers, Animal Control, Humane Society, and all the neighbors we could think of, to see if the pigs belonged to them or anyone they knew.

Rick, my son, was working up the road a couple of miles away, so we couldn't reach him. If we had somebody taking a video, I'm sure we would have won big bucks on America's Funniest Home Videos.

Finally, I recognized the roar of Rick's old truck coming toward home, so I went out to the road and began waving and hollering for him to hurry. Because of my wild gesturing, he thought for sure Kim had gone into labor. After he learned the real cause of my excitement, he joined the chase. Hearing the commotion Elverda and her husband, Bob, arrived. Now there were five of us chasing pigs-a very pregnant woman, one overweight man, one short fat granny, and two senior citizens, with two wide-eyed kids standing on the sidelines.

We eventually got one pig locked in a vacant shed by enticing it to follow a bucket of food. Rick cornered the other pig, grabbed its back foot, and tied it to a tree with a scrap of rope. By this time, the yard looked like World War III. The garden and raspberries were a mess, most of the laundry was off the clothesline and trampled, and the kid's swimming pool and toys were history.

We thought the excitement was over for one day. We all adjourned to our own kitchens for dinner and a bit of rest. Suddenly, the phone rang. The people housesitting for the Hansens, who lived about a mile down the road, had come home and found their pigs gone. They called the State Troopers. Luckily, someone at the station happened to remember us calling earlier. The Troopers told them where they could find their escapees. The owners walked over and herded them home. The pigs marched ahead of them like obedient children. I couldn't believe it. The caretakers gave Kim and Rick fifty dollars to replace the kid's ruined swimming pool and battered toys. They also treated us both to a healthy share of pork that fall.

OUR ALASKAN OUTHOUSE
Darlene Robinson

n 1948 we moved to Alaska and settled on a homestead at Mile 23 of the Glenn Highway. Of course there was no electricity, and that meant no running water. Water for all our needs had to be hauled to our home from a nearby creek or from neighbors. I arrived the first week of May but Bruce, my husband, had been there three months and had our house (all 12 by 24 feet) ready to move into. In Alaska, a house is ready to move into when you have walls and a roof. He didn't have an outhouse ready for us, but set right to work on it. It was about 6 by 8 feet which is a large outhouse. The walls went up to about four feet and there was no roof. Snow and rain was a big problem, and I hated sitting there, looking around. A couple of times, we had callers surprise me, which was a very uncomfortable situation. We had this outhouse for the first year. If you planned to go out there, you always took a broom to sweep the seat.

When our neighbor was digging his potatoes that fall, he chased a bear over the windrow and it stayed around our house for a couple of days. I wouldn't let the two babies out, even when I was with them. I was afraid to go to the outhouse. Bruce, being his funny self, brought some fire-crackers home and told me to light a few when I needed to go outside and the bear would leave. Then he told all the neighbors when they heard the firecrackers not to worry, it was just me going to the outhouse!

The following year, Bruce built the nicest little outhouse of anyone in the neighborhood. It was about 5 feet square. It had walls up to the roof that kept the weather out, with a door that kept the animals out. By this time, we had a dog, so I felt safe to work in the garden. Our children were two and three by then, and loved to play outside. Bruce built a two-holer outhouse, a low seat for the girls and another one for adults. He sanded and painted everything, had toilet seats on both holes and it was very clean.

One day the girls began screaming and I ran from the garden where I was weeding, to the outhouse where the noises were coming from. "Oh no," I shrieked. Linda had dropped her dolly down the hole. I tried to console her to no avail. I could see the doll a little way down where it landed on a very narrow ledge. Finally I got the fishing pole, and with a grim face, began fishing for the dolly. I was successful and after a thorough cleaning, the doll was fine. After noticing the smile on this little girl's face I knew I had done the right thing.

After our first winter, I ordered a chemical toilet from Sears to use during the worst weather. In the winter, I always made three daily trips outside. First, I took the waste water and poured it far from the house, then I took the garbage to the burn barrel, and last I carried out the pail from the chemical toilet to the outhouse. When my sister-in-law moved into Spenard, an Anchorage subdivision, I went in for a visit. I washed dirty clothes at her house, gave the kids a bath in a bathtub, and explained to them about the toilet with water in it. When I flushed it the first time, my daughter, Kathy stuck her little head almost into the toilet and said, "Where did you dump that?" Maybe we should go to the city more often.

OINKER
Elverda Lincoln

How do two women keep the bored-housewife syndrome from entering their lives? My daughter's husband was working on the Alaska pipeline. His employment schedule was such that he worked twelve-hour days for one week and then had one week off. My husband worked nights as a meat cutter on Elmendorf Air Force Base. Linda and I knew if we didn't get a project going we would go nuts.

Early that spring in 1974, we applied for jobs in an open-air produce stand in the Anchorage area. After interviews we were told we would probably be hired and to wait for a telephone call. The first of June we went to work as relief checker and stocker for two days a week. As is usual in a business of this type, there is always a certain amount of produce not fit for human consumption.

Because of this we purchased "Oinker," a thirty-pound seven-week-old weaner pig. She was brought home in a gunny sack, the only way to control a squealing, squirming pig. The shock of leaving her first home was too much for her and she immediately caught cold, with the typical symptoms of a runny nose and watery eyes. We made a trip to the local veterinarian and in three days she was her old self again, thanks to a shot. The first week she wouldn't let anyone touch her, but the hands of friendship could not be ignored forever.

Her home was a small, low, abandoned building which our husbands remodeled as best they could. They repaired leaks in the roof and erected a good board fence high enough to discourage any possible escape attempts. A gently sloping ramp, built so Oinker could get from her house to her pen, was added to her remodeling job. The "Hog Hilton" was elegant according to hog standards. It had running water when it rained!

Oinker was a terrible guest. She tracked mud into her home, turned her water container over, and spilled food all over the floor. We had to provide her with room service every day.

With the purchase of pig starter grain, a sack of dried milk, a couple boxes of cull bread from the bakery, plus a ton of rejected potatoes, Oinker grew like Alaska chick-weed. She must have spent many happy hours sleeping and dreaming of the fruit and vegetable goodies she was getting from the produce stand. Our gardens added to her daily smorgasbord.

Each day we worked we put a large box under the produce counter and as the produce crew came across any delec-table pig feed it was chucked into the container.

When Oinker heard footsteps she came running to the fence to see what we had for her; that is, if she wasn't too lazy to get out of her warm bed which was kept in A-1 shape with the occasional addition of fresh straw. Pigs delight in having their sides massaged and scratched and Oinker was no exception. This act shows their trust, love, and contentment. She became such a pet that when anyone came near her she would lie down and want that person to scratch her belly.

By late September the produce stand closed down for the season. It was time for Oinker to go to piggy heaven. Both husbands informed us emphatically that neither one of them would butcher Oinker. They were too chicken to do the job, so Oinker went to the Palmer slaughterhouse. It was no easy undertaking trying to load a 300-pound animal into a two-wheel trailer. Gentle persuasion could not entice this porker to walk up the sloping ramp. The air in that vicinity soon hung heavy with smoke consisting of rantings, ravings, cussing, and swearing, as two strong men tried to coax a pig into the trailer for the final trip of her life. After watching this fiasco I buffaloed my way between the men and the pig with a partly filled bucket of grain. Oinker put her snout into the bucket and as I calmly and slowly moved backwards up the ramp she followed, not realizing she was being tricked. She dressed out at 222 pounds.

Bob, a meat cutter by trade, cut up the meat to our satisfaction. Hams, roasts, and chops were all custom cut. We made twenty-five pounds of pork sausage, as well as thirty pounds of link sausage, and rendered out six gallons of lard which was used for pie crust and baking powder biscuits. This was my first and only attempt at making head cheese and it was a complete disaster.

Scraps, bones, and cracklings rendered from the lard went for dog feed. The skin with fat remaining on it went into a recycled turkey net and hung on a nail on our deck for the birds. We kept a detailed list of all expenses incurred in raising Oinker. She cost us 67 cents a pound. Prices of pork products in grocery stores, at that time, were in the general range of $2.00 to $2.50 a pound.

Our pig raising project was fun and profitable too. Maybe we would raise two pigs the next summer.

NOT YET
Myrtle Gislason

Many years ago my husband and I and our nearest neighbors, formed a working unit to operate a large dairy farm. This partnership was a success until my husband passed away. Then more responsibility rested on my shoulders. We decided to hire a milker. On his day off we took over the milking chores.

We worked hard day after day. One particular night I went to bed about eight o'clock. The following day was our day  to do the milking. I woke up and decided I would surprise Bob by helping set up the milking equipment and herded the cows into the holding area. They were reluctant to enter but after much prodding and encouragement they finally cooperated. When I finished I planned to notify him everything was ready for milking.

I left the barn and started back to the house, went by the neighbor's house and rapped on the window (our houses were close together) to let Bob know everything was ready. I didn't hear anything. Finally the lights came on in the kitchen. Then it came to me, "I bet I got the wrong time." I headed for home and telephoned Bob. It was twenty minutes after twelve.

I apologized to Bob and said, "I'm sorry. I'll go back to the barn and shut everything off. You can go back to bed now. I am so embarrassed."

I never lived this event down.

NORTHERN CHICKENS
Elverda Lincoln

In 1953 we moved from our small cabin to a three-room house two miles south of Wasilla. A large Quonset hut sat forlorn in the yard. After many months of looking at this hut through my kitchen window, I judged the time was right to put this lifeless building to good use, a perfect home for chickens. One hundred laying hens, purchased from the local farm supply store, would bring the shed to life, keep me busy, and supply my family with eggs and meat. We'd sell extra eggs to offset the feed bills.

Keeping the baby chicks warm and fed consumed most of my days and nights for about a month and a half. They devoured sack after sack of chick mash, a mixture of vitamins, ground grain, and other growth-stimulating ingredients. They soaked up warmth from the heat of an oil-burning brooder stove borrowed from a neighbor. The brooder is built like a large umbrella close to the floor, with a heater in the center, and fueled with oil from a barrel located nearby. The tiny chicks soon learned to get under the umbrella to stay warm.

The attention these yellow fuzz balls demanded kept me busy in many ways I didn't think possible. For a while, it was like caring for a new baby. Any sudden movement set the peepers into a panic, causing them to promptly pile up in a corner and suffocate. Keeping the brooder stove too cold was just as much a catastrophe as keeping it too hot.

The baby chicks ate themselves out of house and home, and soon grew to fryer size. Separating the hens from the roosters was a way to eliminate the number of star boarders. The roosters ended up in the frying pan as Sunday dinner.

By fall, the hens were ready to lay eggs. My husband and I made nests and roosts for them. I threw straw and an occasional scoopful of sawdust from our woodpile on the droppings and floor to the delight of the chickens. The hens spent the winter singing and scratching in the sawdust and straw, eating mash, and drinking warm water.

They apparently took pleasure in eating snow from my boots, so I kept a shovel near the hut door. Whenever I entered their domain, I shoveled some snow on top of their litter. This served a double purpose; the hens were happy with this treat and it kept the path to the hut clear of snow.

They laid plenty of eggs and were just as content when it was snowing or raining as when it was minus 20 degrees. Egg-gathering time became a routine chore. A few hens complained with loud raucous squawks about the invasion of their nests. Some dared me to take eggs from under them and protested with well-placed pecks. Friends, neighbors, and the local grocery store bought every egg I could spare. After the feed bill was paid I still had enough money left to purchase groceries.

After the kids were in bed for the night, my husband helped me cull the hens. With a gunny sack and a flashlight, we quietly and cautiously made our way to the hen house. Bob measured the distance between the hen's pelvic bones—two fingers wide, an indication of a good layer. Two hens at each culling session was all I could handle. I canned many quarts of fat, large birds.

During one of our culling sessions, twelve hens were crated for processing the following day. I knew this would be a tiresome and long job, so I offered a good friend a deal she couldn't refuse.

"If you come over and help me dress out these fryers tomorrow, you can take two home for dinner," I offered. She willingly accepted this challenge. With her four children and my two, we divided our time between settling kid's fights and dressing out the fryers. By late afternoon, with two live roosters in a gunny sack, my friend and her four young ones went home happy with their prize.

A few days later, when we stopped by her homestead on the way to the grocery store in Wasilla, she greeted us at her door. Excitedly she told us, "I thought you gave me two roosters. Yesterday, when I butchered them, I found what looked like eggs in them."

Grinning broadly from ear to ear, my husband exclaimed, "Those were roosters all right. Were there two eggs in each of them?"

Then it dawned on her what the two so-called eggs were. Her face turned beet-red and quickly changed the subject and invited us in for a cup of coffee and cinnamon rolls fresh out of her oven.

My chicken venture lasted two years, kept me in touch with adults and caught up on valley news, and gave me some pocket money too.

My family never tired of custards, French toast, deviled eggs, angel food cake, and homemade ice cream. I fried, roasted, and stewed chickens, and also canned some for use with dumplings.

Using an eight-quart pressure cooker to can chicken was a learning experience for me. I was afraid the cooker would explode, but by keeping a close watch on the dials, I soon became an expert on the use of this marvelous invention.

A neighbor friend tried to can chicken with a pressure cooker, but her attempts were disastrous. She was distracted and didn't realize what could happen if the arrow on the dial crept past the red danger zone. Excess pressure built inside the cooker, which caused the safety valve to explode. Chicken then escaped through the small opening and ended up on her kitchen walls, even on the ceiling. It took days for the poor woman to clean up the mess. Her new pressure cooker ended up in the garbage dump and she did no more canning.

An old-timer told me of a Matanuska Valley family with three children, who had a fish camp across Cook Inlet to which they retreated every summer, taking enough provisions to last the season.

The one item they missed most at the site was fresh eggs. One year they decided to take eight laying hens with them to the camp. Their boat was loaded with a dog, two adults, two children and other needed supplies. The hens were crated for the long trip across the Inlet. The weather was warm and sunny when they left. Halfway across the open water a sudden squall came up and soaked everything, especially the two sacks of grain for the hens. Upon arriving at their destination, unloading began. The two sacks of grain were spread on the beach above tide line. This was done in hopes the bright sun would dry out the soggy mess. The warm sun shining on the grain soon caused it to ferment. Since the hens hadn't eaten for a day, they quickly gorged themselves on the wet feed.

A few days later the hens staggered up and down the beach, drunk as could be, to the amusement of family members, who scooped the grain up off the beach and made other arrangements to dry it. For the rest of the summer, they enjoyed fresh eggs.

NEVER AGAIN
Margaret Heaven

n the early 1970s I decided to raise some chickens, for meat and eggs. We had some cats and a young collie shepherd dog. Chukra, our cherished, canine creature was our family pet. She never bothered our other barnyard creatures or ventured far from home.

Chukra got the wandering fever when she was two years old, and proceeded to investigate the neighborhood. At five o'clock one summer morning I got a phone call from my neighbor, Lu, who lived a mile west of us.

That conversation went something like this:

"Margaret, this is Lu. Is your dog at home?"

"Um, I think so. Just a minute." I walked to the kitchen door, opened it and called Chukra. I hurried back to the phone.

"Lu? No, she doesn't seem to be here. Why?" Visions of my beloved dog lying hurt or dead along the side of Fairview Loop Road filled my mind.

"Well, your dog was here with two other dogs, killing our chickens."

"No! It can't be Chukra. She's never done anything like that. Are you sure it's her?"

"Yes, I'm sure. They're just leaving here and they have killed five of my laying hens."

"OK, I'll be right over."

I quickly donned my bathrobe, started my car, and hurriedly drove over to Lu's farm. Embarrassment and concern enveloped me. I didn't blame Lu if she became angry with me. We had been the best of friends and neighbors for many years. We also had weathered many experiences, both good and bad.

I had heard the best way to break a dog of killing chickens was to tie a dead chicken around its neck and tie the dog to a tree, away from the house, for at least a week. You just can't keep either a chicken-killing or an egg-sucking dog around. I sure didn't want to get rid of our dog. So I went to Lu's and got one of the dead chickens.

On the way home, I spotted Chukra and two other dogs running across one of the nearby fields. There were indeed five dead birds in Lu's chicken yard.

When Chukra got home she actually looked guilty. I never did learn to whom the other dogs belonged. I fastened the dead chicken to her collar, took her dog chain and her bowls for food and water out beside the big cottonwood tree behind the house, and chained her up.

After about three days that chicken was getting quite ripe. It was hard to go out and feed the dog. Flies were beginning to stay around her all the time. The dog was looking and feeling quite pathetic. At five days I couldn't stand it anymore. I knew she was punished enough.

I unchained the dog, took her rancid-smelling collar off and threw it and the chicken carcass in the burn barrel. The dog stunk to high heaven of rotten chicken, so I had to give her a bath. It was awful! The stench was overwhelming and quite hard to destroy. It took several baths to remove the odor.

The punishment worked. The dog didn't pay any attention to chickens anymore. That is, until about a week later, when we came home and she had one of our chickens in her mouth, half-eaten.

I was so upset I grabbed the dog and the chicken. I yelled at her and called her "bad dog." Then I beat her with that dead chicken until all I had left in my hand were two chicken legs. There were chicken parts and feathers everywhere. When I finished I screamed and yelled at the dog and cried because I knew we'd have to get rid of her.

The dog limped away from me, hid out for half a day, then came home very cautiously. During that time we contemplated what action we should take concerning the future of Chukra. We ultimately decided we would give her one more chance. She lived another ten years and never again killed a chicken.

MOVING BRANCH
Carol Stewart

In 1970 we moved to the Knik area of the Matanuska Valley where we had bought land and were in the process of building a home. That fall the weather was horrible, wet, and rainy. I was cooped up in a cab-over-camper with three kids and a husband who was always in the way.

Late one afternoon I walked across a small trail on my way to the nearby creek, listening to the rain and happy to be away from the confinement of the camper and from the family. I looked at the bushes and wondered which berries were edible and when they would be ready to pick.

Suddenly, I stepped on a branch, and it slid out from underneath my foot. While regaining my balance, I realized I'd stepped on a moose leg. It jumped up, looked over its shoulder and took off down the trail. I made a quick turn-around and raced back to the camper.

The kids looked at me and said, "What's the matter, Mama?"

"Never mind." I gasped. "You wouldn't believe me anyway."

"Come on, tell us. How do you know we wouldn't believe you unless you tell us," my husband commented.

"I just stepped on a moose," I said breathlessly.

"Oh, you didn't either," he said.

That was my first encounter with a moose.

THE MIGHTY HUNTERS
Elverda Lincoln

Frank and Leo, good friends and neighbors, made plans to go on a moose hunting expedition into a remote area of Alaska. They spent hundreds of dollars on equipment: warm clothes, good footwear, new rifles, hunting licenses, food, and airplane transportation. They talked and dreamed of the success they knew they would have on this great Alaska adventure.

While the men were on their safari, Frank's wife shot a big bull moose who wandered into their yard. She used an old 30.06 rifle the men had considered useless. With the aid of good neighbor men, the moose was hung from a block-and-tackle contraption strung between two trees.

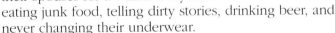

The two women enjoyed their two-week vacation away from their husbands. They went shopping in Anchorage, ate in restaurants some of the time, visited with friends and relatives, attended movies, slept late and kept housework to a minimum. They surmised that the men were actually interested in shooting moose, but also in getting away from their spouses for a while. They'd be eating junk food, telling dirty stories, drinking beer, and never changing their underwear.

When the two hunters drove into the yard, with nothing to show for their two-week effort, they were shocked beyond belief at what they saw. Olive, the small, dainty wife of Frank, was standing on the porch, still in her pajamas, her hair disheveled, a hole in the toe of her slippers, and a wide smile on her face. The butchered moose hung in all its glory between two nearby trees, waiting for the arrival of two strong husky men to turn it into steaks, hamburger, and stew meat.

MEMORIES OF A SHOPPER
Elverda Lincoln

Some people love to shop, others don't. Some have money to shop, others don't. Me, I have a ball. At times I wonder why it is I who gets the shopping cart with wheels that go bump, bump, bump. Or stand in the checkout line behind a customer who waits until she is told how much her bill is before she digs her checkbook out of her purse. Then she asks who to make the check out to and what date it is. First, of course, she asks the clerk for a pen.

On one of my frequent trips to Wal-Mart, as I was standing in the checkout line, an elderly man was playing his harmonica while the clerk checked his items: jeans, western hat, and shirt. He planned to attend a western dance the following Friday and was also looking for a good Christian woman to be his wife. "Do you know of any?" he asked us. People listened and gathered around as he continued to play more tunes. He said he enjoyed life to the fullest and looked for adventure every day. He said he didn't want to die. God was everywhere. He didn't want to go to heaven; he was scared of heights. He played more tunes as the clerk and I tried to talk him into applying for a greeter job right there at Wal-Mart. We agreed a harmonica-playing greeter would be a novelty. The clerk got his name and phone number, and promised to talk to the store manager.

A few weeks later as I was standing in the checkout line at Carr's grocery store the clerk admired my sweater. I told her I had washed it the day before, that was why it looked so nice. We laughed. She told us about an eighty-seven-year-old lady and her daughter in her checkout line. The clerk had admired the older lady's sweater, and the elderly woman said, "You can have it when I'm finished with it." Two weeks later, the daughter returned with the sweater. Her mother had died. When the clerk received the sweater she cried and cried.

She also told us how she admired a customer's blouse. The customer said she admired the clerk's blouse, so they went to the store's restroom and traded blouses.

A few months later, I was in the checkout line at Safeway. A clerk there was yelling at an elderly man in the next line and said to him, "You sure drive slow. I couldn't get around you all the way to Wasilla. I was almost late." The man loudly proclaimed, "I'm retired and in no hurry. Don't tell me how to drive. You drive your way, and I'll drive mine." The clerk yelled back, "I could walk faster than you drive." He responded, "That's fine with me."

The days were warm and sunny but the nights were quite cool. Conditions were ripe for mice to start finding a warm home for the winter and a few found my basement. I made a trip to Wal-Mart and purchased some d-CON, the most popular poison on the market to get rid of mice. While standing in the checkout line, a man asked me where I had found the poison and traps. He had also been looking for that section, but couldn't find it, so I informed him. He noticed I was buying d-CON and proceeded to tell me in no uncertain words that using d-CON was cruel and inhumane. Mice caught in live traps in his garage were taken to the woods and released. They had a right to live and were just trying to find a good home for the winter. I told him if that was the way he felt, I would try to catch mice and bring them over to be released in his basement. He wouldn't tell me where he lived. End of conversation!

One winter morning, after an overnight snowfall, I took a broom and swept the steps of my home, when all of a sudden, the bottom part separated from the handle. To solve the problem, I drove to Wal-Mart to purchase a new broom. I couldn't find the right section, and as usual, there was no clerk in sight to help me. Finally, another customer steered his cart in front of me with a broom in it. I asked him where he'd found it. The customer pointed in the general area, but I still had a hard time finding it. But eventually good luck came my way. I looked at all the varieties available and was shocked at the prices. They ranged from seven to thirteen dollars, give or take a few cents. A young fellow was stocking that section. I commented to him, "I haven't bought a broom for many years. Fifty years ago I could buy one for less than a dollar."

The stocker smiled and answered, "You lived at the time when they made really neat cars."

THE MAGGOT SANDWICH
Elverda Lincoln

Bud, a good friend of ours, went caribou hunting with two buddies of his. They were successful, so Bud gave us a portion of the meat. Since he knew we liked heart, he gave us one. His wife brought this delicacy to our home, cleaned up and ready to cook.

Our family enjoyed cold heart sandwiches with lots of mustard. Two days later I cooked it and planned to make sandwiches for Bob, my husband and Roger, my son. For a reason, I don't remember, the girls must have taken a peanut butter and jelly sandwich on this particular day or they bought a school lunch. I planned to reheat a small amount of casserole from the previous night.

When Roger came home from school that day he asked me, "What were those white things in my sandwich?" He tried to explain, but I still didn't know what he was talking about. I took the remaining heart out of the refrigerator and made a thorough inspection. I considered myself a good cook and knew how to prepare delicious meals from wild game. I was appalled and shocked to find maggots. I had thoroughly washed the heart. I couldn't understand how the maggots stayed inside the cavity.

After thinking hard and long, I finally concluded what happened. Eggs had lain inside the cavity. Insect eggs cling to a solid object for a better chance of survival. Evidently, a second thorough washing did not remove all the eggs. Two days in the refrigerator had allowed the eggs to hatch.

Roger let me know he didn't eat his sandwich since he suspected something was wrong. He told me he'd thrown his sandwich in the wastebasket.

When Bob came home from work that evening we questioned him. He didn't know what we were talking about. Roger and I explained and came to find out Bob had eaten his heart sandwich and enjoyed it. From that day forward, whenever I was at a loss as to what to make for lunch I asked Bob if he wanted a "maggot sandwich."

LIFE ON THE FARM
Elverda Lincoln

era was the first close friend I made upon arriving in
Alaska in 1950. Her husband Bud worked with my
husband Bob installing a telephone line in a remote
part of the state. They shared rides when they returned
home for a weekend now and then. They became close
friends. I visited with Vera during the week. She was lonely
and complained she didn't have anything to do with her
time all week.

She liked chickens and since they had just moved to a
farm, I suggested she acquire some, just a small flock to
keep them in eggs and maybe have a few to sell to help
pay for feed. This she proceeded to do, and in a few years
she was really in business. At one time they had thousands
of hens. The work involved in this operation became too
burdensome, so Bud quit his job, and turned all his attention to running the chicken ranch, wheeling and dealing.

Vera was a small, feisty woman. She had a quick temper
but could be kind as well. Once when she was angry at
Bud, I saw her throw a cube of soft butter on the floor,
splattering it all over the place. Another time I was watching her cook lunch for Bud and two hired men. She

opened a large can of tomatoes, divided it and fixed it three different ways: a third for Bud with no changes or additions, a third for a hired man who liked his with bread in it, and a third for the other hired man, who liked his mixed with macaroni.

Through the years she complained incessantly about Bud. Finally I had enough of her whining. One day I said to her, "If Bud is so bad why don't you divorce him.?" She replied, "What, and give everything I have to another skirt?"

One day Bob went to their farm to purchase some eggs. Arriving there he noticed Bud chasing three wayward calves around the farm lot, not making any headway at getting those critters back where they belonged. Bob joined in the fracas, both men running to and fro, hollering and cussing. Naturally, the calves got excited and weren't being cooperative at all. Finally, they managed to herd the calves near the barn and in order to keep them from going around the building Bob stepped off a wooden plank and fell into a deep chicken manure pit. He was covered with you-know-what from his face to the bottom of his boots—a sight to behold! Vera was watching all this and had tried to tell him not to step off the board, but I guess Bob hadn't heard her.

Anyway, she and Bud rescued Bob from his surroundings and she marched him to the house. There she pushed him into a shower located on the back porch, literally undressed him, and dragged his clothes outside on the lawn. Then she gathered up a complete set of Bud's clothes, which were far too large for Bob, and gave them to the cleaned-up helper.

When Bob came home and entered the kitchen, I said to him, "Where have you been? You have someone else's clothes on." I then listened to his tale of woe. He said the worst part of this ordeal was being thrown in the shower and stripped down to his birthday suit by a strange woman. Bob said Vera was more embarrassed when he fell into the trench than when she undressed him! She threw his dirty clothes in her washer and returned them to him the next day.

This was one of those days Bob should have stayed in bed.

JUDY'S STORIES
Judy Fielding

As a child I went fishing with my aunt and uncle and their three children on the Russian River on the Kenai Peninsula. After a picnic lunch, two of the kids went to sleep on the riverbank while my uncle and I fished. We worked our way upstream, then remembered we didn't have a gun with us, so I volunteered to return to get one. On the way back my four-year-old cousin raced passed me, screaming as he ran from our camp toward my uncle. I intercepted him to find out what was wrong. He didn't say a word, just kept screaming. Suddenly a bear crossed the path between us. The big creature startled me. I dashed back to camp, grabbed a gun, and hurried back to my uncle. By then the bear was far away. He probably was more afraid of us then we were of him.

A few years later two ladies from Utah came to visit. One of the things they wanted to do was pick blueberries, which were extra large that year, and there were plenty of them. We took a picnic lunch and drove to Hatcher Pass in the Talkeetna mountains above Wasilla. We found a spot where the blueberries were so thick it looked like a dump truck had dumped a big load of them. After picking awhile I went back to the Suburban to get my 44 pistol. The ladies stared at the gun and one of them asked me why I was carrying a pistol. "Look around," I told her and pointed at bear tracks and droppings. "See there, they've been eating berries." When I turned around the ladies had high-tailed it back to the Suburban.

My two sissified friends ate lunch while I picked. They went home with empty buckets. I told them they weren't going to get any of mine. That was the end of their dreams of gathering blueberries in the Last Frontier.

The next year my friend Karen and I were going to pick highbush cranberries so we could make jelly. We each had two little kids we took with us. The berry patch was about a mile and a half from my house along the power line, where we parked our truck. As we picked berries among the bushes and trees, I had this feeling in my chest like something was wrong. Being afraid, I reached down to get my gun. It wasn't where it should have been. I thought I must have left it at home but continued to pick awhile longer. The feeling got stronger and stronger that I shouldn't be there. There was no doubt in Karen's mind that I was scared. We gathered up kids and headed toward the truck, looking over our shoulders all the way.

We raced for home and ten minutes later the boy down the street excitedly told us he was walking the power line when a black bear appeared out of nowhere. I knew then the feeling I had was real, and I was thankful we'd returned to the house.

That same fall all the members of my family, including three kids, went berry picking along the Denali Highway. Bud, my husband, scouted around and located the berries for us. We picked while he ate berries and was a lookout for bears, because he had the gun. We followed him from berry patch to berry patch. Always cautious, we kept looking over our shoulders for bears. None were ever seen, but I am sure they were there.

My good berry-pickers are all grown up now, and we fondly remember the good times we had picking berries and worrying about bears.

I WANTED A SALMON
Mary Harvey

One day in late summer my teenage son and daughter and I decided to check the arrival of salmon in the river at our church camp. Traveling south from Wasilla, about six miles off the main road, the lane opened to a wonderful place consisting of some buildings and a bridge across a fast-flowing stream. It was fun to stand on the bridge and watch the salmon go upstream to their spawning grounds.

Luck was with me. I saw at least thirty salmon clustered under the bridge, resting from their ocean journey. I quietly lowered my fish line into the water, so I wouldn't frighten them. They weren't interested in the worm on my hook, so I had to think of another way to get at least one of these silver beauties.

I went to the dining room of the camp, grabbed a baseball bat from the recreation area and returned. With all the strength I could muster, I hit the center of this resting mass. The fish scattered upstream. When I hit the water it was as if I had hit a cement wall. I struggled to keep from falling backwards. Not a single salmon was left in the pool, and if I hit one, it was still able to get away.

My kids decided that if I want a salmon that bad, they'd go upstream to a shallow spot, to see if they could catch one. Soon they returned with a nice specimen which we enjoyed for our evening meal.

It was the best-tasting salmon I had ever eaten, even if I didn't get it with my baseball bat.

HOOKS AND LURES
Joyce Cook

It was the first day of king salmon fishing season. Richard, my husband, and I drove to the Ninilchik River on the Kenai Peninsula. It was a three-hundred-mile round trip. I'm not a fisherwoman, but Richard said he would give me instructions on how to catch fish. We could only fish a mile up from the mouth of the river. The rest of the river was protected and restricted by the Fish and Game Department. When we arrived, hordes of people were lined up on both sides of the riverbank, shoulder to shoulder and elbow to elbow, a process commonly known as combat fishing.

After some simple instructions, I cast my line into the water. My hook got caught on a man's boot on the opposite shore. Next, I managed to hang my line up a tree. Richard had to cut my line so I could continue my sport. Then my line drifted downstream and got caught on something under the water. After Richard rescued my hook for the third time, he cut my line again. I knew I was in trouble by the look on his face. I was embarrassed and mortified. There was no doubt Richard was unhappy with me. By this time I was getting into his large stock of varied and treasured hooks.

Then Richard said to me, "This is it, Joyce. I'm going to find out why the hooks are snagged." So he waded out into the water. I watched him pick up a big object. He tugged and struggled as he brought it ashore. It was a sandbag studded with hooks and lures of every kind. Someone had probably planted it there to make a big haul of hooks and lures at the end of fishing season. Up to this time, no one had waded out to find what was causing the hooks and lures to get caught.

People came over and claimed hooks and lures they said belonged to them. After three men tried to claim their loot, Richard wised up and said, "Hey, if you wanted your hooks, why didn't you try and retrieve them yourself?"

We suspected all along some of the men were lying and thought they were entitled to grabs. You know how it is. Everybody in Alaska is an entrepreneur, but my Richard is the smartest of them all.

FRIGHTENED MOOSE
Jeanene Buccaria

During the harsh winter of 1990 in the Matanuska-Susitna Valley of Alaska, heavy snowfall drove scores of moose from the mountains in search of forage. Some starved and moose calves born that spring were particularly vulnerable. Moose were accidentally killed by motorists. Being prone to choosing paths requiring the least effort, between two and three hundred moose were struck by trains as they traveled along the railroad tracks, attempting to avoid deep snow.

Aware that moose can be dangerous, my ten-year-old daughter Mary and I kept away from them. However, on one occasion we strolled along a narrow trail and inadvertently disturbed a cow moose that had bedded down nearby. The startled animal fled into the woods. Angered by our intrusion, it suddenly changed direction and darted into our path. She charged toward us with her neck lowered and hackles erect. Its intention was clear. This was not a threat. We were about to be trampled. There was no escape route. I reacted with a piercing scream, not knowing the instinctive shriek would thwart the attack. The frightened moose retreated.

In spite of the harrowing experience, I could sympathize with the hostile beast. Its behavior was understandable, since she was deprived of the security of a secluded resting place. Perhaps the hardships the moose had endured that winter were partially responsible for its ill-temper.

I related the incident in a letter to my eldest daughter, Robin, who was attending Middlebury College in Vermont. Robin shared the distressing news with co-workers where she had a part-time job in a dining hall for fraternity men. Seeing humor in the situation, some male employees who were also students, put a Styrofoam cup on a counter with a sign, requesting donations for Robin's pitiful mother and sister. In the student's version the women had become hospitalized after a brutal attack by a moose. The perilous saga became more embellished each time the young men repeated it. They visualized an enraged moose comparable to an elephant in size, violently rushing forward with steam coming from its nostrils, forcing frantic Alaskans to make an unsuccessful attempt to jump over a nearby fence. Their broken and bruised bodies would be discovered later and rushed to an emergency room as lights flashed and a siren announced a warning to other drivers.

The dramatic narrative may have been entertaining, but apparently it wasn't convincing. Only a few coins were deposited in the cup.

FRIENDLY PEOPLE AND MOSQUITOES
Mary Harvey

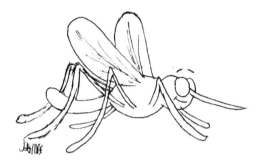

I had often read about Alaska people and how very friendly they were. When at last my family made the move to Wasilla, I was impressed with this friendliness.

While we were building our cabin, people walking into town waved as they went by. Since I came from southern California, to me this was unusual. If your neighbors there even spoke to you, it was a blessing. Later, when I was working in my garden, people passing by still waved. It didn't take me too long to find out they weren't always waving, but were trying to scare away mosquitoes. The mosquitoes were friendly also, looking for fresh blood to dine on.

In Alaska there's a saying, "There isn't a single mosquito in Alaska, they're all married, and they have hordes of KIDS."

FRIEDA AND THE GOOSE
Carol Stewart

Friends of ours had too many ducks, so they gave me a mallard we named Frieda. We acquired her in the fall, she did great through the winter, but in the spring she disappeared for three weeks. When she returned, she was trailing a brood of little ducklings. I guess she met this wild male duck who flew in once a year and then took off again.

Frieda became tame and talked to me in her own ducky way. She'd come up on the deck, bob her head up and down begging for food prattling away with her "quack, quack, quack."

Then I said, "Who's there?"

"Quack, quack, quack."

"Do you want some food?"

Frieda would bob her head up and down. She taught her babies to do the same. It was pretty noisy at times.

Frieda got along well with Dominic, our dog and with our cat. It was heartwarming to see them all get along so well together. The duck met her demise the following spring. She had her nest on a small island in the middle of Crocker

Creek on our property. Every day I went to the creek to feed her and figured she'd come back to my yard in the fall after her little ones were raised. One day I went to the bridge near her nest and called her. No answer. A pile of feathers and shotgun shells was all that remained.

To add to the menagerie, at Easter my husband brought home two cute, soft, round little balls of fluff, who followed me everywhere. Soon these goslings were eating my poppies, lettuce, and anything else they could get their little beaks on.

One day, my son Jay, still in droopy, sagging diapers, was outside playing. The gander decided he didn't like it when Jay got too close to its mate. The gander ran up to little Jay, and grabbed him by his "wee-wee," pulling and tugging. The poor kid was scared and screamed bloody murder until I rescued him. Jay was in pain, so I decided to take him to the doctor in Palmer who said the boy would be fine. The doc couldn't stop laughing when he heard my story of the irate goose. I was so angry at that animal that when I got home I caught him with my bare hands and without thinking wrung its neck. The main course for dinner that evening was goose.

Since I had killed her mate, the surviving goose hated me. I finally had to give her to the Petting Zoo at the State Fair, where kids went into the fenced area to pet her, without problems.

One day, as I was watching the kids at the zoo, a man was standing next to me enjoying the scene also.

"Have you ever seen a mad goose?" I asked him.

He shook his head, "No."

I said, "Watch this. Here goosey, goosey, goosey." The gander hissed, beat his wings and attacked the fence in front of me. Geese do not have short memories.

DOMINIC
Carol Stewart

I n 1970 we purchased land near Knik, and by 1972 we were in a position to have many animals. The first one we inherited was a Great Pyrenees dog we acquired from some people who lived near a park at Finger Lake. The kids who played there teased Dominic, the dog, which made him mean. One day our dog nipped the leg of another small dog. The owner came to our house and told us if we didn't control our dog it would get shot. The kids cried because they thought I would have to shoot Dominic, but they promised to keep him chained.

When he belonged to his previous owner, he slipped his chain, then made his way to the Tastee Freez at Four Corners, to patiently wait for an ice cream treat. One day after he came to our house, the dog took off up the hill toward Knik on the Knik-Goose Bay Road. That was the wrong direction for the Tastee Freez.

Once I discovered he was gone, I drove up and down the road, looking for him. Soon I found him and said, "Dominic, there aren't any ice cream parlors around here. If you want ice cream, you go home." I turned the car around and went home, leaving him sitting beside the road, watching me.

I placed a small dish of ice cream near his dog dish. He never ran away again. After that, whenever the family had ice cream, Dominic also got his share.

CYRUS AND BLESSED
Carol Stewart

Our friends knew we loved animals. A six-week-old piglet, that had been stepped on by its mother, had a hernia, and was blind in one eye, joined our family pets. The vet removed the injured eye, sewed the lid shut, fixed the hernia, and castrated the little fellow, all at the same time.

We acquired Cyrus the middle of May, it was still cold at night. Jack, my husband told me I couldn't have any more animals in the house because of my experiences with them he was not to happy about. The piglet's home was a dog crate, parked outside and covered with old quilts to keep it warm.

"What is that out there?" my husband said when he came home from work.

"Oh, that's the pig I took to the vet and he did all the surgeries and said if it lived, I could pay the bill, and if it died I wouldn't have to pay anything."

My husband brought the pig in the house and placed the crate over the heater in the kitchen. He turned the heat up to about 80 degrees and went to bed. Early the next morning the piglet woke up and squealed in his high-pitched voice. This scared my two-year-old son, who crawled out of his crib, leaped into our bed, and hid under the covers. He wouldn't sleep in his own bed for a couple of weeks, until the pig was moved outside.

That fall I was Superintendent of the Livestock Barn at the State Fair. Cyrus took the Purple Rosette for the Feeder Pig Division. Good care and good food had paid off, though the lady who had given him to me was angry and said I got the winning ribbon because I was a special friend of the judge.

On the first day of the Fair twin goats were born. They were so cute, so tiny and thin. One stayed near its mother and was as happy as could be. The other was forever going through the slats of the pen, causing me to chase it down to return it to its mother. By the conclusion of the Fair, I had talked the owner out of the goat.

That blessed goat was always into mischief, so we named her Blessed. Every two hours she had to have two ounces of milk, even during the night. Whenever I made a trip to Anchorage she rode in the back seat with the kids. When I arrived there I put a leash on her and walked her around for a bit. One little kid said, "Mommy, mommy, look at that funny-looking dog."

I kept the goat in the house until about the first of October. The weather turned cold and rainy and the goat wouldn't go out. She urinated on the floor and from then on was put out in the barn with all the other animals.

CAMPGROUND PORCUPINE
Phyllis Hassinger

Harry, my husband and I had employment as camp
ground hosts at Denali National Park. Sitting for six
hours in a car caused me to make a mad dash to the
outhouse as soon as we arrived there. When I walked
inside a porcupine was chewing on the wood around the
toilet seat. They crave the salt left behind by human con-
tact. They have even been known to eat up ax handles. I
returned to our campsite. People were there from all over
the world. I said to two women who had a campsite near
ours, "Have you ever seen a porcupine?"

"Oh, no", they said, "We have never seen a wild porcupine."

"Go over there to the outhouse. There's one there," I said.

We all trooped to the detached bathroom. The women
opened the door—no porcupine. It was in the spring of the
year and the pit was half full of water. They looked down
into the dark, deep hole and saw one frantically swimming
in circles. The creatures were about the size of a small
beaver, and looked like pincushions with thousands of
quills. The women were furious and said, "You shouldn't
let a porcupine in the toilet where they could drown."

"We didn't let them in," my husband told them. " They chewed their way in. You can't keep them out. That's the way it is."

About an hour later a maintenance man came around, so I told him, "We have a job for you. There's a porcupine in the toilet pit and we have to get him out."

The man got a rake, reached down the hole and fished it out. By that time the spiny critter had drowned. With gloved hands he grabbed it by the tail, and said to a lady, "Do you want a porcupine for breakfast?" The guests there had a good laugh over this.

It was almost impossible to convince the crowd porcupines were edible and tasted like chicken.

Not long after that another one of these prickly beasts woke us up early one morning. He was making noise by chewing on something on the bottom of our motor home.

Harry jumped out of bed to chase him away. When he did this the porcupine climbed to the top of a nearby spruce tree. Soon the maintenance man came by and asked what was going on. A park ranger on his routine rounds stopped also. Harry informed both of them what all the commotion was. The ranger decided he would climb the tree and get the porky down. When he was halfway up the tree, not an easy feat because of the narrow, close branches, Harry yelled to him he should come down. If the animal fell, the ranger would have a major medical problem. The ranger took his advice and climbed back down the tree.

I was watching all this commotion from a short distance and came up with the idea to get the water hose and spray him. The men did this and the porcupine immediately came down. Three men were able to coax him into an empty garbage can with the lid securely fastened. The ranger released him several miles east on the highway where he could do no more damage.

BUGS, SNAILS, AND PUPPY DOG TAILS
Maureen Kelly

*I*t seems children, rather than play with toys, now collect and trade them. There are so many to be had and they are so easily acquired they seem meaningless as far as developing imagination. Back in the "old days" people collected stamps, gems, old coins, and the like. As collections grew, so did knowledge.

In the 50s when I was a nine-year-old, we Cobb kids didn't have extra money for collections. We didn't have many store-bought toys either. We did have trees, grass, and pieces of lumber, but mostly each other.

Later in the 60s our mom decided her daughters needed to have a collection of some kind, so at Christmas specific articles for each person were unwrapped. She thought Debbie ought to collect glass horses and I glass dogs. We collected a few and they gathered dust on their glass backs. We thought they were boring.

My first real collection, however, consisted of seashells, and water-molded glass and smooth stones from the Pacific Ocean. One Christmas I received a beautiful shadowbox for my treasures. Along with this gift I received a cellophane-wrapped box of brightly colored shells and corals. I remember how feminine I felt placing these in the shadow-box along with a glass birthstone doll.

When I was a teen my interests changed from inorganic specimen collections to organic ones. The first victims were the flies who got trapped in my hot upstairs bedroom. I found a clear small marble and discovered it greatly magnified antenna and wings.

Because of this experience I began a collection and a study of anything that flew, from monarch butterflies to praying mantis larvae. Once I found a giant beetle large enough to fill up the palm of my hand. This huge black beetle was sitting on gravel and I wondered why it was so exposed to danger. After picking it up and turning it over, I found out. Another bug had invaded its body and the larvae were devouring it while the beetle still lived. This was a little revolting, but by this time in my life, I had seen many natural things and was teaching myself reverence and respect for all of nature's needs.

I took this beetle home and let the larvae finish cleaning the shell of the beetle, and added it to my growing collection of flying insects. Stick pins were used to mount them and I made labels. As a young adult while preparing to move to Alaska, I stored them in a large cardboard box stuck in a storeroom in my mother's hot, dry attic because I didn't have room for them in my already overloaded station wagon. Later I learned my mother went into the attic to clean and cursed me up and down for leaving a box of horrible bugs in her house. I laugh every time I imagine her opening that box! That was my first experience with someone being bothered by a collection of natural things.

The next bother was with the mailman. I had found a dead baby badger in the woods. The badger's body was also being cleaned by the creature cleaners of nature and I needed to watch the process closely to make sure the cartilage didn't get damaged, so I would have an intact skeleton. At this time I was living in a cluster of fourplexes with individual mailboxes by each door. Needing a place out of sight of neighbors and nosy dogs I put the decaying body in the mailbox. I wasn't expecting any mail for a few weeks anyway. One day I did find mail. I felt sorry and embarrassed for the mailman. I wondered what he thought of my wonderful find and what tale he related to his fellow employees when he returned to the post office.

While house hunting with a friend we happened upon a dead turtle. The owners had tried to let it hibernate under their trailer in a box lined with glass insulation. I surmised the turtle must have inhaled some of the insulation, which caused its death. I asked the owners if I could have it; they readily agreed. I wanted it for the skeleton. I hid my treasure and myself in the bushes, along with two bottles of hydrogen peroxide, Clorox, and a saw. Maggots were already at work cleaning out the body, which I would have liked them to continue, but the turtle would never fit in the mailbox for safekeeping. Trying my best to keep my reverence for life, for the sight was mighty gross, I prayed for help and a strong stomach. I dumped all the disinfectant in the body cavity, then sawed through the bony hinge which connected the top shell to the bottom. In amazement I saw how beautiful the colors of each organ were, and how alike they were to human organs. Even more interesting the turtle's backbone wasn't inside its body flesh as ours, but was joined to the inside of the top of the shell.

Though I tried to hide myself in the bushes to be discreet I was still discovered by children. I dug a hole and buried the flesh, then boiled the shell until it was clean. I am afraid word got around as to what "the lady upstairs was doing." After that children brought me many things to look at, even a tiny baby bird skeleton which to this day I keep wrapped in an antacid box.

When I was a camp director a friend and I were scouting out a trail when we came across a large porcupine that had been hit by a vehicle. I wanted some quills so we stopped our station wagon. I grabbed a spare tennis shoe and slapped it on the porky until the bottom was filled with quills. We laughed at that for years. I decided it would be very interesting to dissect this critter and share it with any young campers who wanted to learn something new about nature. My friend wasn't very excited about this but at my insistence she begrudgingly helped me lift it onto the tailgate to load it into our vehicle. We deposited the carcass under some bushes at the edge of the campground. Somehow word got around and the squeamish camp president found out, because word came back to me that someone had disposed of it. Nothing more was said. I was very disappointed, and I did get some odd looks from some adults. The girls thought I was weird, but they also brought all kinds of things for me to look at, including a dead bat.

I think one of the funniest things that ever happened to me and one of my collections took place when I moved from Juncau to Fairbanks. We had stopped off in Haines to stay the day with some friends who lived on a rocky beach of Cook Inlet. A dead sea lion had washed up on shore and my friend was anxious for me to see it. It was a wonderful sight. It was quite far along in its decay, so much so the skeleton was showing. Because of so much oil in the animal's flesh the bones were beautifully stained a reddish brown. Unfortunately, some stupid lawbreaker person had axed the sea lion's head to take the ivory tusks. Some whiskers, teeth, and stained bones were all that remained. I filled two gunny sacks with these items to take home to bleach. Some of these bones had rather ripe flesh on them. To avoid the smell I tied them to the back fender of our little Volkswagen Rabbit.

Off we went to Fairbanks. The cooler with our meals was in the back. Every time we opened the door, air was sucked into the car with an audible whoosh. Whoever was waiting in the car always got a lung full of that horrible decay smell. There was no shortage of complaints.

The worst and most humorous part of this trip took place a few hot days later in the interior of Alaska. We stopped to put fuel in the gas tank, and an attendant came out to assist us. One whiff and a curious look at the lumpy bags tied to the fender sent him inside. Another customer drove up, and while he was gassing up his vehicle, he noticed more and more flies were appearing. "I wonder why all the flies," he said. "I don't know," I lied. We left laughing until our sides ached.

For a few months I kept my bones on top of the meter and telephone box on the side of the cabin we were renting in North Pole. Dogs kept stealing them until finally all I had left was one whisker.

Now, many years later, in a shadowbox made of old barn wood are various sizes of eggs, moss, skulls, shells, stones, seed pods, dried starfishes, and different types of bird nests, reminders of wonderful things and wonderful times.

BEAR WATCH
Joyce Cook

I n 1992, after an extended absence, my husband and I decided to return to Alaska via the Stewart-Cassiar Highway, a rough dirt road. This highway was an alternate to the Alaska Highway. We were proceeding to Hyder, a small coastal community, located about twenty miles off the main highway when we were blessed with a flat tire on our truck camper. Richard, my husband, changed it.

Though we were traveling with friends, at times we were miles and miles from each other. Sometimes we were in the lead and sometimes they were. Soon our friends came by, and since none of us had eaten, I invited them inside our camper for breakfast and a visit before we continued on our separate ways.

After a few miles we saw a black bear crossing the road. Richard put his head out of the truck window to see better and heard air coming from another tire. Now we had no spare and it was miles to the nearest service station. Richard removed the tire and as he was doing so, the bear sat under a tree and watched the process. It appeared to be more curious than threatening. I kept bear watch. The creature didn't move. Richard left for the nearest service station, rolling two tires down the road. I didn't know when, or if, I would ever see him again.

Before he left, he gave me instructions to rotate the two remaining tires still on the truck. Fear and anxiety filled my body as I was left alone in bear country. Well, I couldn't be blamed if I waited until this large furry beast left, could I? Our friends from breakfast soon came by and again I got to keep bear watch while they rotated the tires for me. I'm so glad that what goes around comes around.

Richard got back that evening, after miles of hitchhiking and bumming rides, but that is another story.

BARN SHOWER
Mildred Ulrich

I t was spring in the Matanuska Valley in Alaska and as usual, mud was everywhere. Our house at the top of a 100-foot hill, with the barn and fields below, commanded a beautiful view of our dairy operations.

One morning my husband came up to the house from the barn and said to me, "Come down to the loafing barn and help me? One of the cows is soon to calve and she's down. We need to get her up and into a dry place."

Quickly I grabbed my barn clothes and we rode the tractor down the hill to the loafing barn. My husband said he would put a rope around the neck of the animal and I should take a hold of her tail. The cow was trying to help herself also, but in her struggles she was useless. All of a sudden the tail slipped out of my hands and I fell in the mud and manure, covering me from head to toe.

My husband, feeling sorry for me and the same time trying to keep from laughing said, "I give up. Let's go to the house."

My reply was, "No, we came to get this cow up and in a dry place, let's do it."

After much pulling, prodding, and tugging, we finally got the cow up on her feet and into a dry place, where she would be comfortable until the birth of her calf.

On the way to the house, we passed a water hose, coiled up on the outside of the milking parlor. My husband grabbed it and sprayed me. There I stood, cold, stinking, and soaking wet.

We rode the tractor back to the house. I raced onto the porch, stripped off all my clothes and threw them into the washing machine.

I assumed somebody might be there because our home was always a visiting place for people. At times, when we came back to the house from the barn, there could be visitors there. Our children had many friends coming and going, and also soldiers from the nearby military base seemed to find their way to our home.

Fortunately, no one was there this time. I headed stark naked for the bathroom and hot shower. Big deal. This was just another day in the life of an Alaska dairyman's wife.

BACKYARD BEAR
Mary Harvey

Early one morning, in the town of Wasilla, where we had just built a small cabin, I was on my way to the "outdoor bathroom." Just outside the cabin a strange noise startled me. I whirled around and saw a black bear not ten feet from me. For a moment I stood frozen, then dashed back into the cabin. It had to be the bear that had broken into our home earlier in the season, upset the sugar bowl, scattered flour, tried to open canned food, and made a mess of everything.

My husband, still in his night clothes, shot the bear, then shot it again before we got up close to make sure it was dead. A neighbor and his wife helped us hang the animal from a strong tree limb for a few days to tenderize it. Bear can be good eating, and we didn't want to waste the meat. We saved the hide, cured it and used it as a rug; since that bear seemed to enjoy our cabin so much he might as well live there forever.

Later on that year, my parents came from California for a visit. I cooked a bear roast for dinner. My mother thought that roast was the best meat she had ever eaten. I didn't tell her what kind of meat it was. If I had told her, she might have lost her evening meal.

BABY
Evelyn McNair

Our Alaska home is cuddled among the trees and willows which thrive along the banks of Cottonwood Creek near Wasilla. Even though our home is not far from the hustle and bustle of Cottonwood Mall and Fred Meyer, we have been visited by moose, ducks, eagles, Canadian geese, and an occasional river otter.

We have a compost pile at our home near our kitchen window. Into this pile go vegetable and fruit scraps, egg shells, bread crusts, leaves, wilted flowers, and grass clippings. The moose who come to visit usually stop by the compost pile for a snack before they amble on.

One summer a cow moose and her young calf came into the neighborhood. Unfortunately, as the cow tried to cross the busy highway, a passing motorist failed to see her, leaving the calf motherless. Our neighbor watched over the young calf and kept it alive.

All that summer the calf stayed in the neighborhood, eating in the neighbor's yard, and then snacking at our compost pile. We learned later this little moose loved apples, broccoli, carrots, cabbage, potatoes, oranges, and chopped up willow. Her favorite treat was bananas, including the peelings. Because she seemed to eat anything we put in the compost pile, it didn't occur to us she might not enjoy some of our scraps.

One morning as I was cleaning the house, I noticed Baby on our deck, looking in the big windows, as if asking for a treat. I took the garbage out to the compost pile, stacked high with carrot peelings, banana peels, potatoes, lemons, and limes. As I watched from the kitchen window Baby hurried over to the pile and started snacking. I continued with my morning chores.

I heard Baby running on the deck. Her head was down, eyes wild, pawing on the deck. She ran and jumped all over the yard. She lowered her head, charged down one side of the yard, back and forth, from one side to the other.

The kids and I watched her behavior, puzzled and laughing at her strange antics. We discussed why she might be acting this way. I thought about what she might have eaten from our compost pile, seriously wondering if she might be choking on something. After bucking up and down for several minutes Baby headed for her home at the neighbor's and we didn't see her for the rest of the day.

A few days later, while speaking to our neighbor, I described Baby's peculiar behavior, and inquired if she had noticed it. She laughed and asked me if anything sour was in our compost pile. "Only lemons and limes," I chuckled.

Baby had never tasted sour food before. From her reaction to this experience it was evident she didn't like that taste and didn't know how to get it out of her mouth.

Even though we continued to toss our limes and lemons on the compost pile, we noticed that now Baby was careful, as she picked through the fruit and veggies. She left the limes and lemons alone.

Baby hung around our neighborhood until late fall. Many moose passed through on their way to other areas. We assume Baby took off with one of them, to do what moose do. Our family thoroughly enjoyed the short time we had with Baby.

ARNOLD
Darlene Robinson

In May 1973 my husband, Bruce, suffered a major heart attack. His working career was over. We had to find ways to supplement our income. In 1974, we and our children had a conference and decided to raise a couple of pigs. Bruce bought some log slabs and some rough-cut 2-by-6s, then looked for a likely spot to build a pen.

We went down a small hill about 150 feet from the house among some birch trees, and began. The trees were used as posts for the pen. A piece of plywood roofed one corner, so the pigs would have a dry spot when it rained. We put some straw in this corner and built a trough of some rough-cut lumber.

Next, we went to a local farmer and bought two pigs. The kids wanted to name them, and after careful consideration, they came up with Arnold. One of their favorite TV programs had a pig named Arnold. They all agreed it was a perfect name. After hours of discussion and argument they finally decided the second pig was Mrs. Arnold.

Everything was going great with the pigs and the girls spent a lot of time with Arnold and Mrs. Arnold, giving them treats from the house. They took their friends to see the pigs and they all scratched their backs, or just watched and visited with them. The pigs were spoiled.

Local grocery stores saved all their vegetable trimmings for us, and we bought grain so the pigs seemed happy and were well cared for. They were growing big when tragedy struck. One was down and couldn't get up and the other one was staggering around.

It was no easy task getting two pigs loaded into the trailer for their trip to the Palmer vet. He couldn't tell what was wrong because they both were fat and healthy. He suggested we take them to the Agricultural College lab to have them examined. The employees at the lab were very interested and asked if the pigs could be left with them so they could observe them more closely.

When we told the girls, they were devastated. They told all their friends the pigs were in the hospital. Two days later the "hospital" notified us that one of the pigs had died but the other one was fine and we could come and get him. The problem was the porkers were poisoned from eating too much insecticide with the vegetable trimmings we had been getting from stores. From that time on, no more trimmings were collected. The kids spent extra time with Arnold. He became even more demanding. He found if he held his head just right, he could look between the slabs of his pen and watch the house. If a car drove up our driveway, or anyone moved up there, he would start to squeal and raise Cain until someone came to visit him. When the family arrived home after a day in town, we often found a note on the door stating the guests were sorry they missed us, but they'd had a nice visit with Arnold.

A friend gave us five hundred pounds of mouse-ruined wheat. Gilman's Bakery in Anchorage gave us a barrel two-thirds full of old powdered milk, and a son-in-law gave us a five-gallon bucket of honey that had spilled in the trunk of his car. All of these goodies were mixed up and became Arnold's main diet. He was a truly happy pig.

When fall came, Arnold was huge and ready for the next logical step. A day was set for him to be taken to the slaughterhouse. When the girls were told, their first reaction was not a positive one, in fact, that would be a gross understatement. After reminding them of our original plan and their agreement to it, they finally came around.

After fighting with Arnold for an hour and a half, we finally tricked him into a trailer and drove him to the slaughterhouse. At midnight the owner phoned us and asked, "What in the world is wrong with your pig? When I turned out the lights to go to bed he started squealing. I went down to see what was wrong. He shut up. I went back upstairs to bed and he started squealing again. This happened four times. I can't get to sleep." I told him Arnold just loved company. He told me later, Arnold was the first pig he killed the next morning.

We had his hams cured, bacon smoked, and sausage made, but whenever the family used the meat, it was never called pork, bacon, or ham. It was always Arnold. He sure was some pig!

ALASKA BEGINNINGS
Koreen Robinson

David, my husband, decided to move to his home state after an absence of a few years. I had always wanted to see Alaska. It had been one of my dreams to tour this great state.

Of course, I had a few questions to ask him. Would we have running water? I could handle anything with hot running water. That would be heaven. Where was the nearest McDonald's? In Idaho this treat was available in the big city, 80 miles away. I would be fine.

A few things in Alaska were quite strange to me. The trees were so thick, you couldn't see your nearest neighbor. I appreciated that. Instead of cows ravaging your garden and yards, moose could wipe out an entire cabbage patch within minutes.

That fall, after my husband had arrived home from his summer employment and before the next construction job began, he and a friend decided to go moose hunting. I had tasted moose burger and looked forward to having all that meat in our freezer for the winter.

I got a telephone call from the union. David had been dispatched to a short job in Cook Inlet. He had to board the boat that evening. I packed clothes I thought he would need, but had no idea what other gear was required. I hoped it was still all together in one spot from his previous job. I was relieved when he and his friend drove into the yard, according to schedule. They had been successful. Two large moose were in the back of the trailer, heads propped up and tongues hanging out. What a sight.

I hurried out of the house and told my husband he had only twenty minutes to take a shower and get his gear together, in order to arrive in Anchorage for his transport to the boat. He looked up at me, stared at the moose, then looked back at me. I can still hear his words, "Whatever doesn't look like steak make into burger."

My mouth must have hit the ground, eyes popped out, and I stopped breathing! What was I going to do? After calming down I noticed the men had the animals skinned and quartered. They arranged the meat quarters in such a way on the trailer that it looked like a whole carcass, with the head and horns hanging over the edge. They thought this was great fun, especially when they observed other drivers grinning and enjoying the scene.

It was comical now that I look back at it. My husband's friend laughed and said, "I'll help you take care of it and I'll bring you the burger."

After a ten day aging period and my inexperienced help and willingness to learn, we managed to process the meat until delectable cuts were safely deposited in freezers. Instructions were given me on how to bone meat, make stew, wrap and mark packages. I was thankful I wasn't anywhere near when the innards were removed. The blood and stench of the warm guts would have made me sick.

I gained much knowledge from this experience which came in handy in the years I have lived in Alaska, the Last Frontier.

I can still see those moose grinning at me from the back of the trailer.

A FOWL ROMANCE
June Robinette

In 1953, my husband, Grady, and I, were freshly settled on 160 acres of virgin land in the Matanuska Valley in Southcentral Alaska. We decided to have some livestock to liven up the place and thought we'd start with chickens. During that first summer, we acquired twenty elderly hens from friends who were culling their flock to be more productive. We fed them some chicken feed and they ran loose around the yard eating green stuff, grass, and weeds, of which we had plenty. Boxes for nesting sites were provided but chickens have minds of their own. We really had to hunt for any eggs we got.

Some time later, Grady was visiting with an old-timer, Jim Kennedy, and mentioned our newest acquisitions. Jim, tapping his snuff box and looking up at Grady, who was a foot taller, shook his head and said, "Do you have a rooster to go with them? You should be ashamed to have that many hens and no rooster. I know someone who has a nice Rhode Island Red they want to get rid of."

Grady drove his rickety old pickup to the owners and said, "Jim Kennedy told me about you. Do you have a rooster you want to get rid of?" Grady returned home with his new prize in a gunny sack.

After a bumpy ride in the back of Grady's pickup, that bird was ready to get out. When he dumped the rooster out of the sack, the wild-eyed critter landed on his feet, looked around and thought he had gone to chicken heaven. He cocked his head to one side and took off after all of them, except one little brown hen who didn't want anything to do with that monster. She lifted her skirts, as if to say, "Oh no, not me!" and dashed around the corner of the cabin so fast he didn't see where she went. I don't think he ever did catch up with that little brown hen.

There was no doubt that rooster was the king of the chicken lot. Whenever I went outdoors to fetch a bucket of water for them, that depraved creature attacked me. In retaliation I hit him with the bucket. He didn't even flinch and never learned to appreciate me.

Two weeks later, Grady and I went to town to replenish our grocery supply. When we returned hours later, we saw evidence a dog had killed most of the hens, but not the rooster. We could see the hero of the chicken yard was beat up, and surmised he had valiantly tried to protect his harem.

The next time on our return from town, we again saw evidence a dog had killed the remaining flock of hens, plus the rooster. I am positive that brave protector gave the dog a run for his money, as the area where the carnage took place was mercilessly trampled down and torn up.

That ended our chicken venture.

ALASKAN BEAR ENCOUNTERS
Judy Shelton

My husband and I, with our two young children and a small dog were traveling in a quiet-running Ford Pinto station wagon on the McCarthy Road, located south of Chitna in the Wrangell Mountains.

We had rounded a curve downwind of a huge grizzly ambling along the road unaware of us. The sound of gravel crushing beneath our tires reached the ears of Mr. Bear. He swung around. Seeing us, he made a fast break into the brush and out of sight.

The real excitement was me! I shouted at my children to get in the center of the car and away from the windows, which I hurriedly rolled up tight. I checked to be sure the doors were locked. My husband commented that bears don't use door handles. I was in full-blown panic.

The camera was on the floor by my feet. I didn't get a picture of my first Alaska bear.

This wouldn't be my only encounter. Over the past twenty-six-plus years I have had many bear sightings, some close-up, and many from a distance.

In 1983, my children and I spent a great deal of time at my sister-in-law's homestead on the McCarthy Road. As the long days shortened, the leaves turned to the glorious shades of orange and yellow, signaling to us that fall was on the way. The creek which emptied from Long Lake filled with spawning salmon. The bears also returned to see if the fish had arrived yet.

That's what happened early one summer morning. I heard a deep growl coming from our dachshund-terrier dog. Although she was small, she had a large ego and no fear of bears or any other wild critters who ventured near the homestead. Neither the dog nor I could see through the curtains to the outside, but we both knew a bear was nearby. Panic seized me. Shivering and shaking, I had to quickly figure how to keep the bear from entering the cabin, devouring or maiming my children.

My sister-in-law's two dogs and mine made all kinds of noise. I awoke my children, gave my eleven-year-old son the 22-250 rifle and had my twelve-year-old daughter hold a handful of 22-250 shells. I had a 22 pistol. The plan was to tell the dogs BEAR, get them excited, open the door, and sic them on the unwelcome guest. Those dogs were no strangers to bears.

My strategy included instructions for my children to flee into the bedroom and out the window should the bear enter the cabin. We hoped we wouldn't have to implement this plan. After the dogs were properly excited, we opened the door and they ran out to tangle with the bruin, who stood shoulder-high to the handlebars of a four-wheeler, located fifteen feet from the cabin door.

True to their nature, the dogs pursued the bear, who ran for the greenhouse, circled the water barrels and returned. I shot at him through a small window. The dogs ran him toward the large food dehydrator in the yard. When they came back I fired the pistol and hollered for the dogs to run the bear off. Away they all ran toward the barbecue pit. They came back again! I fired several more shots and gave the dogs a firmer command to chase the marauder away. This time they sent the trespasser down the trail and into the brush. Much to my relief, a few minutes later they returned unscathed without Mr. Bear.

About a week later a grizzly was killed down by the creek after attacking a dog and charging its owner. As near as my children and I could tell from the description the shooter gave us, it wasn't the same bear. We will never know for sure. Our Mr. Bear never returned.

My last episode was one that shouldn't have been all that exciting except to me. I awoke early in the morning, used the powder room and sat down on the couch to ponder the activities of the day. Recently, we had been having lost dogs wandering through our yard. When I heard noises outside the house, and saw a black paw on the window sill, I sat up straight and said, "Now, whose dog is that?" As I said that, I looked into the muzzle of a small black bear looking back at me through the window.

Panic grabbed me and I jumped backwards to keep the bear from touching me. I said, "Oh shoo! Get out of here!" It kept looking at me. I grabbed the phone, which was located next to the window, and called my neighbor, since my husband was working away from home. So was her husband. I phoned another neighbor. No men there either. I phoned my brother who lived a mile away. He would be right over as soon as he got dressed.

I tried to keep my eyes focused on the bear after he finally got off the window sill.

Oh no! My poor birds! I had a flock of more than fifty chickens and turkeys in the backyard. What is a little chicken wire to a bear? I used an old standby, my voice, yelled out the window at the bear and told it to get out of there.

Help soon arrived. First, my brother came and we retreated to the backyard with firepower. The bear was gone. A turkey walked nervously around the outside of its pen trying to get back inside with the others. The bear had attempted to enter and apparently gave up after getting entangled and escaping from a fishing net hung from the top of the enclosure. The turkey took flight and exited through a hole in the fishnet. Soon she was herded back inside with the other birds.

Next, my neighbor arrived with her young son and a gun. They were happy the bear had left the premises. Soon another neighbor arrived ready to dispatch him. All were sure from my description it was the black bear that was orphaned the previous fall. It was somewhat stunted and made its living getting into garbage and raiding yards and sheds. After everyone returned to their homes, I resolved to keep my wits and rifle handy, since there was a real chance that the hungry animal would come back looking for a meal.

My husband reminded me that during my summer at the homestead, I was constantly in the midst of bears and never got as shook up as I did over one small blackie. He was right.

Frozen
Mary Knutson

In the 1970s my husband was gone from home for weeks at a time working on the Alaska pipeline. My kids were all grown and living their lives away from home. Women like me were known as Pipeline Widows.

Since I was left alone with lots of free time I spent a great deal of it with my sister-in-law who lived about a mile and a half away. One winter evening I was playing cards with her and other members of her family. Around midnight I returned home. In order to drive into my own driveway I had to back into a small parking area. It was so small that if I didn't do this I had no way to get out.

A bull moose was standing in my garden munching on abandoned cabbage and broccoli. I didn't pay any attention to him and proceeded to back into the small parking area. As soon as I got parked, I turned off the engine. In an instant the windshield was the only thing between me and the moose. My car was a Volkswagen bus, the engine being under the vehicle, so you see the moose could have kissed me except for the glass between us! He wouldn't let me out of the bus and he wasn't about to move off to greener pickings. He stared and I stared. I didn't know what to do. It was no use honking the horn or screaming. There was no one around to hear me.

It was 20 degrees below zero. I didn't dare start the car to keep warm. I figured if I did, the noise of the engine might startle the moose into an attack. I waited and waited for the moose to vacate the area. I got colder and colder. I couldn't get out of the bus on the driver's side, run around to the back of the vehicle and into the house because the moose wouldn't let me.

Sitting there in the cold I had to think of something. I climbed over the front seat into the back, opened the double doors and ran for the house. I don't remember opening the unlocked door.

When I could breathe again, I warmed up and went to bed. The next morning the moose was gone and life returned to normal.